DOGGY DARE

Also in the Animal Ark Pets series

1 Puppy Puzzle
2 Kitten Crowd
3 Rabbit Race
4 Hamster Hotel
5 Mouse Magic
6 Chick Challenge
7 Pony Parade
8 Guinea-pig Gang
9 Gerbil Genius
10 Duckling Diary
11 Lamb Lessons
12 Doggy Dare

LUCY DANIELS

Doggy Dare

Illustrated by Paul Howard

Hodder
Children's
Books

a division of Hodder Headline plc

Special thanks to Mary Hooper

Text copyright © 1998 Ben M. Baglio
Created by Ben M. Baglio, London W6 0HE
Illustrations copyright © 1998 Paul Howard
Cover illustration by Chris Chapman

First published in Great Britain in 1998
by Hodder Children's Books

A Catalogue record for this book is available from the
British Library

ISBN 0 340 71374 7

Typeset by Avon Dataset Ltd, Bidford-on-Avon, Warks

Printed and bound in Great Britain by
Mackays of Chatham plc, Chatham, Kent

Hodder Children's Books
a division of Hodder Headline plc
338 Euston Road
London NW1 3BH

Contents

1   The newcomers   1
2   Mystery solved   9
3   Something surprising   19
4   Biscuits and bones   29
5   Mixed feelings   43
6   A wonderful trick   55
7   Training troubles   71
8   Bad news   83
9   Clever dog!   93
10   Doggy disgrace   101
11   Scruff to the rescue   111

Contents

1. The newcomer
2. Nursery school
3. Some things can't fix
4. Biscuit and ball
5. Winter holiday
6. A wonderful trick
7. Tania's birthday
8. Big top
9. Clever dog
10. Doggy daycare
11. ...to the rescue

1

The newcomers

Mandy Hope stood outside Welford's post office with James Hunter and his Labrador, Blackie, frowning slightly. "Who's that?" she asked, nodding towards a boy standing on the other side of the road.

James undid Blackie's lead from the railing it had been tied to. He looked over to the boy and shook his head. "I don't know," he said. "I've never seen him before."

The two of them stared as the boy across the road glanced at a comic, then stuffed it into a bag he was carrying. Mandy was all ready to say hello, but the boy didn't look over at them. Instead he walked off, crossing the road further up the High Street.

"It's no one from school, is it?" Mandy said. "No one I recognise at all."

"He's probably just a visitor," said James. "Honestly, Mandy, you are nosey!"

Mandy smiled. "I just like to know what's going on!"

The two friends stood on the pavement, ready to cross the road, and James patted his side for Blackie to sit down next to him.

"Sit, Blackie," he said. "And look carefully before you cross . . ."

But Blackie didn't sit. Instead he jumped up and shoved his nose into the bag of lemon drops that James had just bought.

"No, you don't!" James said. "You only get a reward if you walk across the road properly, keeping to heel."

"You'd better not let him have too many sweets," Mandy said. "They're bad for his teeth."

Mandy's mum and dad were both vets – as Mandy hoped to be one day. In the meantime, she loved animals to bits and had as much to do with them as she possibly could. James always said that there wasn't a pet in Welford that Mandy didn't know by name!

"They're bad for *your* teeth," James said, "but that doesn't stop you eating them, does it?"

"That's different," Mandy said.

On the other side of the road James gave Blackie a doggy treat for being good. He golloped it down in one, then looked hopefully at James for another.

"Not yet," James said. Apart from trying to save Blackie's teeth, James was trying to train his dog to be obedient. If Blackie did what he was told, then he got a doggy treat as a reward.

Mandy looked up the road. "There's that boy again," she said. "He just went in the greengrocer's, and now he's come out."

"Let's catch him up and talk to him," James said. "He might be new here."

"Yes, perhaps he – oh, he's got a dog!" Mandy said in delight, as a small, scruffy mongrel suddenly appeared out of the shop doorway and began to walk behind the boy.

The boy stopped and spoke to the dog, then bent to pat him.

"I don't think I've seen that dog before, either," Mandy said.

"There's a mystery for you, then," James said, popping a lemon drop in his mouth and offering the bag to Mandy. "A strange boy, and a strange dog."

Blackie leaped for the paper bag again and knocked it to the floor. James had to sit him down and tick him off. By the time Mandy and James set off again, the mystery boy was almost at the end of the

High Street. He was about to turn into a lane that led to one of the farms.

"He must be a stranger," James said. "If he wasn't, he'd know not to go down there. With all the rain we've had lately the lane's a swamp. A bit further down the mud's really deep."

Mandy nodded. "My dad said that only tractors could get through to the farm now." She screwed up her eyes in order to see the small figure more clearly. "And it doesn't look as if he's wearing wellies, either."

"Come on," James said. "We'll tell him about the mud."

They broke into a run and quickly reached the top of the lane, Blackie leaping beside them.

"Hey!" Mandy called after the boy. "Don't go down there!"

"Come back!" James yelled.

The scruffy little dog who was following the boy turned and put his head on one side, as if listening to Mandy and James. But the boy just carried on his way.

"You'll get stuck!" Mandy called.

"You can't get past the mud!" James cried. Even Blackie joined in with a couple of woofs, though he didn't know what he was woofing at. The scruffy dog stopped and looked round again when he heard Blackie bark, but the boy didn't even turn.

"Well!" Mandy said.

"That's a bit rude, don't you think?" said James. "Ignoring us like that. I mean, we're only trying to help."

Mandy shrugged. "Oh well," she said, "he'll find out for himself soon enough about the mud. What a strange boy . . . I wonder who he is."

"Maybe he just doesn't want to be friends," said James.

"I think his dog does, though," said Mandy.

James laughed. "That's just the sort of thing you *would* say, Mandy Hope!"

2

Mystery solved

Mandy didn't think any more about the boy and the dog until the following Monday at school. Mrs Todd, Mandy's teacher, finished calling the register and put it to one side.

"Now, I've got some news for you," she said to her class. "We've got a new boy joining us this morning."

Mandy looked round the class. There wasn't anyone new there yet. And she hadn't seen anyone in the playground earlier, either.

"His name is Joey Appleyard," Mrs Todd said. She glanced at her watch. "I've asked him to come in to join us ten minutes late today because I wanted to speak to you about him first. He's a rather special boy, you see."

The class sat up and listened carefully.

"Joey is deaf," Mrs Todd said. "Which means we've all got to be a little bit more thoughtful and a bit more helpful."

Gary Roberts put up his hand. "Can he talk?" he asked.

Mrs Todd nodded. "Yes. He can speak perfectly well. He's only been deaf for about two years. He learned to speak in the usual way when he was a baby. His speech sounds a little bit strange now, though, because he can't hear what he's saying. So I don't want any of you to make fun of him."

She looked round the class. "Now,

after half-term there'll be a learning assistant here. She'll help Joey understand the instructions that I give. Until then, I think it would be best if he sits at the front of the class. He can face me, on Mandy's table." She smiled at Mandy. "And I know you'll help him as much as possible, won't you, Mandy?"

Mandy nodded, pleased to be asked.

"Now, I want you all to treat Joey just like you treat the rest of your friends," Mrs Todd went on. "All you've got to remember is to look at him when you're speaking to him so that he can read your lips. Try to speak very clearly, and don't stand behind him and talk, because then he won't be able to pick up a thing."

She crossed to the classroom door. "I think I see him outside in the corridor now."

The children shifted in their seats, craning their necks, eager to see this new boy.

Mrs Todd ushered Joey in and everyone stared at him, feeling just slightly disappointed because he didn't look any different at all. He looked just like anyone else. He was average height – just a bit taller than Mandy – with short brown hair and ears that stuck out very slightly.

When she saw him, Mandy gasped in surprise. It was the boy who'd been in the High Street on Saturday. Of course! *That* was why he hadn't turned round when they'd shouted – because he hadn't heard them!

"This is Joey," Mrs Todd said, her hand

on Joey's shoulder. She led him over to Mandy's table.

Joey watched Mrs Todd's lips as she spoke slowly and precisely. "Joey, this is Mandy. She'll show you round the school at lunch-time and help you if you get stuck with anything."

"Thank you," Joey said. He had a rather loud, harsh voice.

"Hello, Joey," Mandy said, slowly and carefully. She felt self-conscious as she spoke, as if she was in a play or something.

"Hello, Joey," everyone on Mandy's table said, speaking clearly and moving their lips in an exaggerated way.

Sarah Drummond burst out giggling.

"That's enough, Sarah," said Mrs Todd sharply. "Don't let's give Joey a bad first impression of us. We hope he's going to be really happy here." She clapped her hands. "Now, we've got English first thing. Let's get our books out and begin, shall we?"

★ ★ ★

By the end of the day Mandy felt that she and Joey were getting on quite well. Sometimes she forgot what she'd been told and spoke too quickly to him, and often he had to ask her to repeat what she'd said. Once or twice she'd even had to write things down, or make signs with her hands. But by and large they seemed to be managing.

Joey was shy, Mandy realised. He hated being stared at; didn't like being the centre of attention at all. This made Mandy feel that she wanted to look after him, and she'd tried to stop everyone crowding around him at lunch-time.

"Where do you live?" she asked him as they walked across the playground together after school.

"Taggart Lane," Joey said.

Mandy nodded. "It's nice up there. It's near where my gran and grandad live."

James was waiting just inside the school gates for Mandy. Being a year younger, he was in the class below Mandy and Joey. Mandy had already introduced the two boys at lunch-time.

"James and I will walk home with you if you like," Mandy said. "I'm going round to see my gran and grandad anyway."

"OK," Joey said.

As they came out of the school gates Mandy gave a squeal of delight. "Oh! There's your dog again!" she said. "He's come to meet you."

"What?" Joey said, looking puzzled.

"Sorry," said Mandy, "I forgot to face you. Your dog." She pointed. "He's waiting across the road for you."

Joey's face split into a grin. "But he's not mine," he said.

"We saw him with you on Saturday," James said, careful to face Joey.

Joey nodded. "He's been following me about ever since we moved in last Friday. He even came to school with me this morning."

"Who owns him, then?" Mandy asked as the dog ran over to them and leaped at Joey excitedly. "Where does he live?"

Joey shook his head. "I don't know.
He just seems to appear when I come
out of my front door."

"He's lovely!" Mandy bent to pick up
the excited, scruffy little bundle of fur.
"I don't know what sort of a dog he is,
though. A bit of terrier and a bit of
spaniel . . . he's got a bit of everything in
him, really."

Joey nodded. "I call him Scruff."

"Scruff's about right," James said,
ruffling his fur, "but he's a lovely dog."

16

Mandy nodded admiringly. "He's really cute." She put the dog down and he danced about Joey's feet. "He hasn't got a collar on," she went on. "I wonder where he's come from? Will you . . . do you think your mum will let you keep him if he doesn't belong to anyone?"

Joey shook his head sadly. "My mum doesn't like dogs," he said. "I think she's scared of them."

"Oh, that's a pity," Mandy said. She bit her lip. "I suppose I'd better ask my mum and dad if they know anyone who's lost a dog, then."

"What's that?" Joey said.

"Sorry," Mandy said. "My mum and dad are vets," she explained slowly and clearly. "We live at the other end of the village – in a place called Animal Ark."

Joey laughed. "Is it really called that?"

James nodded, and added, "And there's not an animal around here that Mandy doesn't know about."

Mandy looked at Joey and Scruff messing about together. "You two really get on well," she said. "Wouldn't it be great if we could persuade your mum to—"

"We'd better find out if he belongs to anyone first," James said hastily. "Before you start giving out pets."

Mandy laughed. "All right," she said. "First things first."

3

Something surprising

Mrs Appleyard – Joey's mum – was standing at their garden gate looking out for him. She had an anxious expression on her face. It was clear she was worried about Joey and wondering if he'd had a good day at his new school.

She saw him coming down the road with Mandy and James and waved and smiled at them; but then Scruff appeared and she frowned.

"Shoo!" she said when Scruff ran up to her. "What are you doing here again? Get off with you!"

Joey, Mandy and James exchanged glances as Scruff ran off down the road. He sat himself on the pavement a short way away, keeping an eye on Joey from a distance.

Joey introduced Mandy and James to his mother, and they stood and chatted to her while Joey went indoors to unpack his schoolbag.

"Welcome to Welford," James said politely. "I hope you like it."

Mandy nodded in agreement. "It's really nice living here," she said. "I'm sure you'll be happy." She was dying to say something about Scruff, but she thought she'd better tread a bit carefully at first.

"Mrs Todd told us all about Joey," she went on. "About how we have to look at him when we're talking and things like that."

Mrs Appleyard nodded. "It's probably going to be a bit difficult for him at school sometimes," she said. "He'll be getting an assistant soon, though – someone to help when he doesn't catch what Mrs Todd says."

"Oh, we're helping with that already," Mandy said eagerly. "Joey's in my class and he's sitting next to me." She smiled. "I'm going to get really good at speaking to him. I have to try to remember to speak slowly and clearly."

Mrs Appleyard relaxed a little. "That's good of you," she said. "Joey had a bit of a hard time at his last school, where some of the children weren't quite so understanding. It's good to think that Joey's with someone who's looking out for him." She looked worriedly up the road towards Scruff. "But if you really want to help you could start by keeping that dog away!"

There was silence. James nudged Mandy. Mandy nudged him back. She cleared her throat. "Actually," she said,

"Joey really seems to like Scr . . . that dog. And the dog likes him, too."

"Yes, but even so . . ." Mrs Appleyard said.

"He was waiting for Joey outside school today," James volunteered.

"Hmm . . ." said Mrs Appleyard.

"He seems quite a sweet little dog," Mandy tried.

Mrs Appleyard tightened her lips. "I don't like dogs," she said.

"Oh, but why not?" Mandy couldn't stop bursting out. "Dogs are lovely. They're really loyal and they stick with you through thick and thin."

"Yes, well," said Mrs Appleyard, "I'm afraid you must allow me to disagree with you about that. When I was about Joey's age, I made friends with a little stray mongrel that seemed as friendly and sweet as this one here. But one day it turned on me and bit me quite badly. I'm afraid I've never been able to trust a dog since."

"Oh, that's really sad," Mandy said.

"Sad because the dog bit you, of course, but also sad that now you don't like *any* dog."

Mrs Appleyard smiled suddenly. "I can tell you're a real animal lover. I expect you've got a dog yourself."

Joey had come outside again now, and he and James began to kick an old tennis-ball back and forth. Meanwhile, Mandy explained to Mrs Appleyard about her mum and dad being vets. "I haven't got a dog, though," she finished, "but James lets me have a share of Blackie. He's a black Labrador and I can play with him whenever I like. And I also get to see all the animals that come to Animal Ark for treatment."

"*Now* I know who you are!" Mrs Appleyard exclaimed. "I've met your grandmother. She came round with some home-made scones the day we moved in. They were delicious!"

"That sounds like Gran all right." Mandy smiled. "She's the best baker in Welford."

The telephone began to ring inside Joey's house and his mum turned to answer it. "You and James are welcome to come round whenever you like," she said. "And will you tell Joey for me that his tea will be ready in ten minutes – and he's not to encourage that dog!"

Mandy promised to pass on the message. While she was talking to Joey and James, the ball that they'd been playing with had rolled into the gutter and gone further down the road.

No one took much notice – and no one took much notice of Scruff going to get it, either, until he was standing behind Joey with it in his mouth. He put it down and began to bark to attract Joey's attention. Joey, who was busy watching Mandy's lips as she was talking, still didn't realise Scruff was there.

Scruff barked on, but before Mandy or James could tell Joey about him, the little dog suddenly put out a paw and tapped Joey's foot.

Joey looked down, surprised. "Scruff!"

he said. "What do you want?"

Mandy touched Joey's arm to catch his attention. "He's brought you the ball back," she said.

Joey saw it, and bent and ruffled the dog's fur. "Good boy!" he said. He picked up the ball. "You're a good dog, aren't you?"

A sudden thought occurred to Mandy and she looked at James, startled. James had the same surprised expression on his face.

"Hey," he said. "Are you thinking what I'm thinking?"

Mandy nodded violently. "Yes!" she said.

Joey was looking at them with a puzzled expression. "What's going on?" he asked.

"Well," Mandy said, 'I don't know how he *does* know, but I think Scruff knows that you can't hear. He started off by barking at you, but when you didn't take any notice he put his paw on your foot."

"Wow!" Joey said. "That's fantastic!"

"What a clever dog!" Mandy said.

There was a knocking from the window of Joey's house and Mandy and James looked round. Joey followed their glance.

"Teatime!" Joey's mum mouthed. She indicated that his food was ready, and beckoned Joey in.

Joey looked down at Scruff, sitting patiently at his feet, then at Mandy.

"What are you going to do about Scruff?" Mandy asked. "Your mum said not to encourage him."

Joey bit his lip, then he grinned. "I might forget that!" he said, and all three of them laughed.

Mandy and James said goodbye and told Joey they'd see him the next day. As he and Mandy walked down the road, James looked back.

"Hey," he said, "look at Scruff!"

As they watched, Scruff squeezed himself under Joey's garden gate and settled himself down in the long grass by the front wall.

"I don't think Mrs Appleyard is going to get rid of Scruff very easily," James said.

"Neither do I," said Mandy. "I think Scruff's already made up his mind where he wants to live!"

4

Biscuits and bones

Mandy was deep in thought when she arrived at Lilac Cottage, where her gran and grandad lived. Mostly she was thinking about Scruff and Joey, and what she could do to persuade Mrs Appleyard to give the little dog a chance.

When Mandy went round to the back of the cottage, Grandad was in the garden picking runner-beans. A basket full of them stood on the grass next to him, spilling out on to the ground.

"I hope you like runners!" Grandad said, peering through a screen of tall bean plants. "I reckon I've still got enough to supply twelve greengrocers here. However fast I pick them, they just seem to keep on growing."

"I love runner-beans!" Mandy said. "And you know Dad does. We'll eat however many you want to give us."

"Good!" Grandad said. He threw a few more beans into the basket and then straightened up. "I'm glad you've arrived, Mandy. I've been looking for an excuse to stop for a cup of tea."

He picked up the basket of beans and they went inside the cottage. "You know your gran," he went on. "She's a real slave-driver. Once I start work in that garden, I'm not allowed to stop without good reason."

"Oh, stop kidding!" Mandy said, giggling.

Gran was pouring boiling water from the kettle into the teapot. She got Mandy a cold drink out of the fridge.

"What news then, love?" she asked. "You look as if you've got something to tell me."

"I have!" Mandy said, giving her a hug. "We've got a new boy at school, and he's sitting next to me because he's deaf and I've got to look after him and tell him things. I have to speak to him very care-ful-ly and prop-er-ly," she said, separating each of her words into syllables.

Gran smiled. "Well," she said, "it may interest you to know that I've already met your new friend. *And* his mum."

"Oh, of course you have!" Mandy exclaimed. "Mrs Appleyard said you went round with some scones."

"She's a very nice woman," Gran said, stirring sugar into Grandad's tea. "She told me that she's a widow and she's brought up Joey on her own. He seems a very nice little boy, too."

"You said his mum seemed a little bit over-anxious about him," Grandad put in.

"With good cause!" Gran said. "He was very seriously ill, you see," she explained to Mandy, "and one of the effects of his illness was that he lost his hearing. He had to have months off school, and then when he went back some of the other children gave him a bit of a hard time. Teased him about the way he spoke."

"I don't really understand why he speaks in such a funny way," Mandy said. "Sometimes he just booms out things and makes me jump!"

"Well, apparently it's something to do with not being able to hear yourself," Gran said. "You forget how to adjust the tone you're speaking in, and you can't tell if you're shouting or not. And you forget how to pronounce certain words, too. And new words are difficult."

"Poor little chap," Grandad said.

"There's something else to tell you, too," Mandy said. "There's a dog that's been hanging around Joey ever since they moved in."

"I saw it," Gran said. "Cute little thing. It was sitting in the front garden when I called. But then Mrs Appleyard chased it away."

"That's just it," Mandy said. "Mrs Appleyard doesn't like dogs. She was bitten by one when she was young."

"Well, not everyone's mad on animals like you are!" Grandad said.

"But this dog seems really good with Joey," Mandy went on. "And he's never had a pet before and he really likes Scruff, too."

"Scruff, is it?" Grandad said. "So you've named him already."

Mandy smiled. "Joey did. It's a sweet little dog . . . and do you know, we think it's already worked out that Joey's deaf." She explained how Scruff had brought back the tennis-ball and used his paw to get Joey's attention.

"Well I never!" Gran said.

"Did you know that they have special dogs trained to do just that?" Grandad said. "Old George – a chap I knew years back – had one. It wasn't a special pedigree or anything, just your average sort of mongrel. It used to let him know when there was someone at the door and so on. Hearing dogs, they call them."

Mandy put down her glass. "I've heard of guide dogs for the blind," she said, "but I didn't know they had special dogs for the deaf as well. What else did old George's dog do?"

"Well," Grandad said, "it's a few years ago now, but if I remember, he just used to do things around the house. Things like letting George know if the telephone was ringing."

"But then what would happen?" Gran asked. "George couldn't hear who was speaking, could he?"

"I think he had a special amplifier on his telephone that made people sound ten times as loud as they really were. Mind you, George wasn't completely deaf; he had some hearing."

Mandy frowned. "I'm not sure whether Joey has or not. But how did George's dog tell him that someone wanted him?" she asked.

"He used to go up and put his paw on George's knee – that was the signal that something was up. And then, when George was alerted, his dog would take him to where the noise was coming from. He'd lead him along to the front door or the telephone or whatever."

"I see," Mandy said. She sat for a moment, deep in thought, then she said, "Do you think James and I might be able to train Scruff to help Joey?"

"To have those hearing-dog skills; same as George's dog?" Grandad asked. He shook his head doubtfully. "I wouldn't know, love."

"I don't think you'd have time to train a dog as thoroughly as that," Gran said. "I mean, look at the amount of time you and James have spent on Blackie, and he's still not exactly top of the class in obedience, is he?"

Mandy grinned. "Sometimes I think Blackie just enjoys being difficult. He *likes* disobeying us," she said. "But Scruff's already got something right all on his own. So if we could only teach him a bit more, then Mrs Appleyard might let him stay."

"You'd better see what your mum and dad have to say about it first," Gran said.

Mandy's eyes sparkled. "But wouldn't

it be great if we could teach Scruff to let Joey know when someone wants him? Like when there's someone at the front door?"

Gran and Grandad agreed that it would. "But don't get too keen on the idea," Gran said. "You might not be able to talk Mrs Appleyard round to letting Joey keep him."

Grandad, who'd been dividing the runner-beans up into piles, suddenly asked, "Does Joey like runner-beans?"

"Now, how do you expect Mandy to know that?" Gran said.

"Well, if you think he does," Grandad went on, "you could take some in to him on your way home. I've had enough beans this year to feed all of Welford!"

Mandy laughed. "I'll certainly take him some, then."

A bit later, with two parcels of runner-beans wrapped in newspaper under her arm, Mandy set off for home. She was going to stop by Joey's house on the way.

Grandad had started work in the garden

again and Mandy paused to talk to him. "I'm a bit worried about Scruff," she said. "I think he's sleeping in Joey's garden and I don't know what he's doing for food. I didn't like to ask Joey about it in front of his mum."

Grandad scratched his head. "I don't know what to advise, Mandy," he said. "It's difficult. If Mrs Appleyard doesn't want the dog there, maybe you shouldn't be encouraging him."

"I know." Mandy sighed. "But he *is* there and he's probably hungry . . ."

Grandad thought for a moment. "You're going to Joey's with the runner-beans, aren't you? So how about taking a couple of handfuls of dog-biscuits with you?"

"That's a good idea," Mandy said.

"There's some in the shed – left from when you were trying to train young Blackie in our garden."

Mandy brightened up. "And I could just accidentally drop them in Joey's front garden, couldn't I?"

Grandad winked. "But if anyone sees you, don't tell them where you got them!"

As Mandy went through Joey's front gate, Scruff came out from his hidy-hole in the long grass beside the garden wall. The little dog jumped at her, pleased to see her.

"Hello, boy!" Mandy said. She bent down to fuss him, then straightened up and looked round carefully to make sure no one was watching. "How about a few dog-biscuits, then?" she asked softly, and she took them out of her pocket and put them in a pile on the grass.

As Scruff started crunching them, Mandy reached up to ring Joey's front-door bell – just as Joey opened the door.

Both laughed, startled to see each other.

"I've come round with some runner-beans from my grandad," Mandy said, and she handed over the newspaper bundle.

Joey thanked her. Then, from under

his jumper, he drew out a chop bone. "I was just coming out here to give this to Scruff," he said.

Mandy smiled, relieved. "I thought you'd be feeding him. He's living in your front garden, isn't he? James and I saw him going under the gate as we left."

Joey nodded. "I've been managing to save him something from most meals." He glanced towards the house. "I don't know whether Mum knows or not. If she does, she's not saying anything about it – and neither am I!"

Mandy smiled. "All three of us, you, James and I, will have to try and get her to change her mind about dogs."

"That would be great!" said Joey. "I'd love to have Scruff for my own pet."

5

Mixed feelings

"Jean, guess what!" Mandy said, bursting into the waiting-room of Animal Ark.

Jean Knox, the receptionist at the veterinary practice, looked up from the papers she was working on. "Don't tell me," she said. "It's something about an animal, right?"

Mandy looked surprised. "How did you know?"

Jean smiled. "Because it's usually something about an animal with you."

"Well, it's not just about an animal," Mandy began, and started to tell her about Joey. She'd got to the part about Mrs Appleyard not liking dogs when she heard a voice saying, " Oh, dear me, no!"

Mandy stopped, astonished.

"Oh, dear me, no . . ." the strange voice said again, and added, "poor Polly!"

As Mandy looked all round, Jean burst out laughing and pointed up at the shelf. "Meet Polly," she said.

"A parrot!" Mandy said, looking up, amazed.

It was indeed a parrot. A fine big one, with bright-yellow breast feathers and striking blue wing feathers.

"Where did she come from?" Mandy asked in awe. She hadn't seen a parrot that closely before, and had certainly never heard one speaking so clearly.

"A man brought her in," Jean said.

"She's losing her feathers. Look at her chest. She's a bit threadbare."

Mandy looked more closely and saw that there was pinkish-grey, rather scrawny-looking skin showing through the parrot's thinning chest feathers. "More like *feather*bare," she said. "Poor thing!"

"She's been booked in for observation and a few nights' stay," Jean went on. "But her owner says she likes being with people, so we're keeping her out here by the reception desk."

"Good idea," Mandy said. "She can

see everything that's going on." She went behind the desk and was about to put her finger through the bars of the cage to stroke Polly, but the bird made a sudden movement towards her. Mandy jerked her finger back quickly.

"No, I shouldn't risk it if I were you," Jean said. "Her owner says she's as friendly as anything, but you never know with birds. She might be feeling out of sorts and fancy a quick peck of a nice pink finger."

"Does she speak much?" Mandy asked.

"When she wants to," Jean said. She pursed her lips. "And when she does, she comes out with a few things that your teacher might not approve of!"

Mandy laughed. She was just about to ask if Jean knew of anyone who'd lost a dog like Scruff, when her mother put her head round the door.

"Mandy! I thought I could hear you," she said. "Good day at school?"

Mandy nodded, her eyes shining. "Lots to tell you, Mum," she said.

"That's good," said Mrs Hope. "Come through straight away, can you? Tea's ready, and it's my yoga class tonight so we can't hang about."

Mandy picked up her schoolbag. "Bye, Jean. Bye, Polly," she said, but though she stood by the bird's cage and said "Goodbye, Polly" twice more, the parrot didn't reply.

"As I was saying," Jean said, "she only speaks when she wants to."

Mandy sat in the dining-room with her mum and dad. As she tucked into her mushroom omelette and salad, she wondered how to bring up the subject of Scruff. Her feelings about the dog were a bit mixed. On the one hand she thought that if someone who loved Scruff had lost him, then it would be wonderful to reunite them. But on the other hand, now that Joey had become so fond of Scruff, it would be terrible for Joey to lose him.

"You know I've just been telling you

about the new boy – Joey," she said after some thought. "Well, there's a nice little dog that's been hanging around him, wanting to be friends."

Her mother and father laughed. "Whenever you take an interest in something, there's sure to be an animal lurking somewhere in the background!" Mrs Hope said.

"That's just it," Mandy said. "He is in the background. Joey's mum won't let him in the house."

Mr Hope finished his meal and put his plate to one side. "Suppose you tell us all about it," he said.

So Mandy did, finishing by telling them about Grandad's friend with the hearing dog.

"So I was thinking," she said, "that if Mrs Appleyard would let Joey keep Scruff, then maybe James and I could teach him some of the things that a real hearing dog would do." She looked anxiously from her mum to her dad and back again. "What d'you think?"

Mr and Mrs Hope weighed up the question for a long moment, then Mandy's mother said, "I really don't think that would be possible, love. You see, those dogs receive months of specialised training."

"Yes, but Scruff's already shown he can do it," Mandy said. "He just seemed to realise all on his own that barking at Joey got no response."

"Well, that's true," her mother said. "If it wasn't just coincidence, of course."

"Well, if he's made a start for himself, I can't see that trying would do any harm," Mr Hope said. "Though I really don't think you should expect too much, Mandy. And you mustn't be disappointed if it doesn't work out."

"But when would you do all this?" Mandy's mother asked. "Training like that takes a good deal of time, and I wouldn't want you to fall behind with your homework."

"Half-term's coming up!" Mandy said. "James and I could go round every day and work with Scruff and Joey then. It would be our project for the week. A doggy dare!"

"Well," Mr Hope said. "I suppose you could try – but only if Mrs Appleyard agrees."

Mrs Hope nodded. "One other thing, Mandy," she said, "whose dog *is* he? He must belong to someone."

Mandy shrugged. "I've not seen him around here before, not ever. And there aren't any LOST posters up."

"Well," said Mrs Hope, "perhaps – before you get too excited about him helping Joey – you ought to put up some posters of your own."

"To advertise Scruff?"

Her mother nodded. "You'll have to ask if anyone's lost a dog of that description."

"But suppose they have?" Mandy said quietly.

"Well," said Mrs Hope gently, "it would be best to find that out before you've trained Scruff, wouldn't it? Before you all get too fond of him. And wouldn't it feel good to reunite him with his real owner?"

"I suppose so," Mandy said a bit glumly, wondering how Joey would feel about that.

"Another thing . . ." Mrs Hope said, "you really ought to be a bit wary of a strange dog that no one knows anything about."

"I was just going to say that," said Mandy's father.

"I know it's not nice to think about, but he could have something wrong with him, some disease or other," Mrs Hope went on. "You wouldn't want him to pass it on to all the dogs in the neighbourhood, would you?"

Mandy shook her head slowly.

Her mother stood up and began collecting up the plates. "I'm off to yoga," she said. "Have I got two volunteers to wash up?"

Mandy jumped up. "Of course you have, Mum," she said. She didn't mind washing up – and anyway, she wanted to get her father on his own . . .

"You know how you and Mum were saying how important it was that Scruff should have his health checked out?" she began as they were putting away the plates and cutlery.

Her father looked at her quizzically. "I don't remember quite saying that."

"Well, you two said we shouldn't get too fond of a dog that we didn't know anything about, didn't you?"

"Mmm . . ." said Mr Hope. He looked at Mandy with his head on one side. "Somehow, I think I know what's coming . . ."

"Well, do you think you could check him over for us?" Mandy said in a rush. "Give him the all-clear? Oh, please say you will!"

Mr Hope pretended to look doubtful. "I don't know about that," he said. "Who would pay for this check-up?"

Mandy bit her lip worriedly. "If you could let us have a special rate, I . . ."

Mr Hope began laughing. "I was only teasing you," he said. "Of course I'll check the dog over. When do you want to bring him in?"

James came round after tea. Mandy told about Grandad's pal with the hearing dog, and filled him in on her father's promise to give Scruff a health check.

"In the meantime, though, I said we'd make some posters," Mandy said. "Mum and Dad both say that we need to make quite sure that Scruff hasn't already got a home."

"I can help with those," James said. "We could do them on my computer at home. I can make posters and invitations and all sorts of stuff on it."

"That would be great," Mandy said. "And there's four days before half-term, so we can put a poster on the bulletin board at school, as well."

The school bulletin board was where everyone pinned up news items or advertised things they had for sale. If you had some books to sell or an animal that needed looking after in the holidays, this was the best place to let people know. Some time back, James had put up a notice saying that he wanted a puppy, and Mandy had seen it and told him about Blackie. That was how they'd started to become best friends.

"You could do the posters and print them out," Mandy said, "and I'll ask Dad if I can borrow his instant camera and get some photos of Scruff to stick on them."

James nodded. "The funny thing is," he said, pushing his glasses back on his nose, "we don't want the posters to actually work, do we?"

"What do you mean?" Mandy asked.

"Well," James said, "we really don't want to find Scruff's owners, do we?"

Mandy shook her head. "Not really . . ."

James grinned. "This must be the only time anyone's advertised something and hoped no one would reply!"

6

A wonderful trick

"Is he OK?" James asked anxiously, as Mandy came out of Animal Ark surgery with Scruff in her arms.

"He's fine!" Mandy said. "Dad gave him a check-up and said he's a fit little fellow. He's a bit underweight, but Dad said he'd soon make that up."

"That's good!" James said.

"And guess what? Dad gave him all his injections, too. And his worm pills and everything!"

"So he's fighting fit and ready to go?"

"That's right," Mandy said.

Once outside, Mandy put Scruff down on the pavement and gave him a pat.

"So all we need to do now is work out whether he can help Joey . . ." she began.

" . . . And persuade Joey's mum to take him in!" James finished.

They began to walk along the road together, Scruff running in front of them. It was the first day of half-term and they were going to meet Joey on the village green. The three of them were going to start trying to train Scruff.

That morning, Mandy had woken up early and gone to collect Scruff, who was still living in Joey's front garden.

Mrs Appleyard, it seemed, was pretending that Scruff didn't exist. Mandy wondered if she was secretly hoping that, in time, Scruff's real owners would turn up and claim him.

"So no one's come into Animal Ark about our posters?" James asked.

"No one," Mandy said. She counted on her fingers. "We put four posters up, didn't we? One at school, one on the green, one outside the post office and one in reception at Animal Ark. And there hasn't been a single reply. No one's even said they've ever seen him before."

"That's all right then," James said with satisfaction.

They neared the village green, chatting all the way. When they turned the corner, they saw Joey standing under the oak-tree.

"Scruff – there's Joey!" Mandy said. The dog looked up at her curiously. "It's Joey! Off you go, boy!"

Hearing the word "Joey", the dog pricked up his ears. He looked all round, and then glanced ahead and must have recognised his friend. He gave a short yelp and began to run down the road as fast as his little legs would carry him.

"Look at him go!" James cried.

"He really loves Joey, doesn't he?" Mandy said.

James nodded. "It would be a real shame if Joey wasn't able to keep him."

Mandy squeezed James's arm. "It's up to us, then, to see that he's allowed to stay."

Joey was smiling from ear to ear when they reached him.

"Scruff knows me all right, doesn't he?" he boomed.

Mandy nodded. "Of course he does," she replied.

"And was he all right? Did your dad say he was healthy?"

"He's absolutely fine," Mandy said. "Nothing to worry about at all. Dad's given him all the injections he needs, too."

"Brilliant!" Joey said. He looked at James. "Why didn't you bring Blackie with you?"

James shook his head so that his floppy hair fell into his eyes. "I thought I'd better not," he said, speaking as clearly as

Mandy had done. "One dog at a time is best for training."

Mandy nodded agreement. "How we want Scruff to behave is different from how we want Blackie to behave. Poor Blackie would get in a complete muddle."

"And he's bad enough now!" James said with a laugh.

"OK," Mandy said. "I think we ought to start with the easiest thing – what we think Scruff knows already."

Mandy had spoken to her mum and dad several times about Scruff's training. They had emphasised that Mandy and James should begin very slowly, repeat everything over and over again, and not try to do too much at once.

"You'll confuse Scruff if you do that," her dad had told her.

"If he does get it right, though, be ready with lots of praise and encouragement," her mum had added.

"So," James asked now, "you mean we should call to Joey and get Scruff to tell him we're calling?"

Mandy nodded and turned to face Joey. "You walk away with Scruff," she said, "and when you're crossing the green, James and I will call you. Don't turn round, though, even if you think we're calling. We'll see if Scruff does anything. If he tries to tell you, give him one of these doggy treats."

Joey beamed. "Sounds like fun," he said. And if it meant that his mum might be persuaded to let him keep Scruff, then it would be just brilliant.

Joey and Scruff set off. "Bye, you two!" he said, just for effect, and Mandy and James called "See you!" and "Goodbye!"

They let Joey get halfway across the green and then shouted "Hey, Joey!" and "Come back here!"

Joey continued walking, although Scruff looked round at them once or twice.

"Come back!" Mandy called at the top of her voice.

"Joey! Joey!" James shouted.

But Joey just carried on walking. Scruff looked round again and then looked up at Joey. As he didn't seem worried, the little dog trotted on.

Joey got right to the other side of the green, then he turned, waved to Mandy and James and shrugged. Mandy beckoned him to come back.

He looked disappointed when he reached them. "It didn't work," he said.

"Never mind," Mandy said. "We didn't really expect it to work that quickly. We'll try again."

They tried again, as before, except this time they shouted even louder; they yelled for Joey to come back. Scruff looked back at them again but still didn't do anything to alert Joey.

The next time, when Scruff heard the children calling, he actually looked up at Joey and gave a couple of barks – but of course Joey didn't hear him.

After two more tries, Joey was getting a bit down-hearted. "Maybe, that time outside my house, he didn't really tell

me that the ball was there," Joey said. "Maybe it was just coincidence."

Mandy shook her head. She was disappointed, too, although she wasn't going to show it. "I'm sure it wasn't," she said. "I'm *sure* he knows. He's just thinking about something else."

"We've got to keep trying!" said James.

But the next time Joey set off and they started shouting for him to come back, Mrs Ponsonby, the rather grand lady who lived in Bleakfell Hall, walked past.

"Well, really, children!" she said. "Such shouting and screaming. Is it really necessary to make such a racket?"

"Sorry," Mandy said. "It's just . . ." She was about to explain when Mrs Ponsonby flapped her hand. "Children nowadays. Really!" she said. She shook her head and walked on.

James and Mandy rolled their eyes at each other. They didn't dare make another sound until Mrs Ponsonby had disappeared into the post office. Joey had got to the other side of the green by then, and had to be beckoned back.

"Sorry," Mandy said when he arrived. "We didn't do that one properly. Let's try again."

The next time they increased their efforts, yelling Joey's name, waving their arms and jumping about like mad. And this time it actually worked! This time Scruff looked up at Joey and barked. Then, getting no response, he jumped up and licked his hand, then pawed at his foot.

When Joey looked down at Scruff, the little dog ran a few steps backwards, towards Mandy and James, then stopped and looked up at Joey as if to say "Look! Someone wants you!"

"Oh!" Joey said, pretending surprise. "I'd better go back." And, giving Scruff his reward, he turned to go back to Mandy and James.

When he reached them, they all leaped around, madly excited. "It worked!" Mandy said.

"He did it!" shouted James.

"Good old Scruff!" said Joey. And Scruff ran round and round in circles barking, not knowing what all the fuss was about but pleased to be part of it.

They made Scruff repeat his trick three times more, to make quite sure it wasn't just a fluke. Now that he'd got the idea of what was wanted, he was able to do it without all the yelling and arm-waving. It just took one or two calls of "Hey, Joey!" for him to pat Joey's foot with his paw, or jump up

and put his nose in Joey's hand.

Once they'd got that straight, James said they ought to make sure that it would work in other places, not just on the green.

"I mean, how many times is Joey going to walk across there?" he said.

So they varied it by having Joey walk towards the post office, and then did it again across the road. A bit after that, Mandy's grandad came by on his way to church bell-ringing practice and they asked him to call Joey.

"We just want to make sure that Scruff will tell Joey when other people call him, and not just us," Mandy explained, and everyone was thrilled when he did.

When they'd covered just about every combination they could think of, and Scruff had eaten his way through a whole packet of doggy treats as a reward, the three friends and Scruff made their way to Joey's house.

They stood on the front step, made Scruff look as unscruffy as possible, and rang the doorbell.

Mrs Appleyard greeted them warmly – then saw Scruff and sighed. "Is he still around?" she asked. "I was hoping he might disappear this half-term."

Mandy cleared her throat. "There's something we want to show you," she said.

"Oh yes?" Mrs Appleyard said warily.

Mandy turned to face Joey. "Off you go, Joey!" she said. "Goodbye!"

"Bye, Joey!" called James.

"Whatever's going on? Where's he going?" Mrs Appleyard asked. "His lunch is ready."

"He's not going anywhere," Mandy said, smiling broadly. "But say goodbye anyway."

Mystified, Mrs Appleyard said goodbye as Joey, accompanied by Scruff, went out of the gate and shut it behind him. He then began to walk down the road.

"Now call him back," Mandy said to Mrs Appleyard.

Mrs Appleyard looked more mystified – and even a little annoyed. "Don't be silly," she said. "He can't hear me."

"Just try it," Mandy pleaded. "And come to the gate and see what happens."

Mrs Appleyard tutted as they walked down to the gate. She called, "Joey!" rather half-heartedly, and then gave a squeal of surprise when Scruff immediately jumped up and nudged Joey's hand with his nose. Joey turned, waved to his mum, and came back.

"Well!" Mrs Appleyard said. "I don't believe it!"

"Do you want him to do it again?" James asked.

"Well, I . . . yes, I do indeed," said Mrs Appleyard, and Scruff and Joey walked in the other direction and repeated the trick.

When they came back, Mrs Appleyard stood for some time, shaking her head in disbelief.

"We think we might be able to teach Scruff other things to help Joey, too," Mandy said.

"So can we keep him?" Joey suddenly

burst out. "Oh *please*, Mum. He'll be no trouble. He's such a good dog. He's brilliant!"

"My dad's examined him and said he's as fit as can be!" Mandy said persuasively.

"Well . . ." Mrs Appleyard began.

"Oh, do say yes," James pleaded. "Joey and Scruff really love each other."

"And Scruff would be so good for him . . ." Mandy put in.

Mrs Appleyard sighed and smiled. "I know when I'm beaten," she said, "and I must admit that what that dog's just done is pretty amazing. He can stay for the moment – but he's on two weeks' trial. If he shows any signs of being aggressive during that time, if there's any biting or snarling or chewing of the furniture, then he'll have to go. All right?"

Joey flung his arms round his mum. "Thanks, Mum!" he said. "Oh, thanks ever so much!"

7

Training troubles

"So how's the dog training going?" Grandad asked a couple of days later. He'd come to Animal Ark to leave another bundle of runner-beans. "Are you making much progress?"

"Scruff's doing really well," Mandy said happily. "We haven't actually tried to teach him anything else yet, though.

We've just been reworking what you saw him doing on Monday. We thought we'd better just go over and over that lesson first."

Grandad nodded. "Good idea," he said. "You don't want to confuse the poor thing."

"Scruff is only on two weeks' trial at the moment," Mandy went on, "so we shouldn't push him too much."

"Joey's mum isn't won over yet, then?" Grandad asked.

Mandy shook her head. "I think she's a bit scared of Scruff, actually. She doesn't say so, but I'm sure she is."

"Well," Grandad said, "you know what they say: once bitten, twice shy."

"No, no, no!" came a sudden loud cry from the other side of the door.

"Whatever's that?" Grandad asked, startled.

Mandy laughed. "That's Polly," she said. "A parrot. Jean's got her in reception with her because she likes company. She's in for observation because she's losing her feathers."

"Bless me," Grandad said. "A parrot, eh? Dead clever, some birds!"

"And some animals!" Mandy said promptly. "Especially hearing dogs."

"That's true," Grandad said. "Old George's dog made the world of difference to him."

Mandy beamed. "And Scruff's going to make the world of difference to Joey!"

"Scruff's only allowed downstairs," Joey said. "Mum won't let me have him in my bedroom. And he has to sleep in the kitchen in a cardboard box."

"But it's a nice big cardboard box," Mandy said, "and at least he's indoors! That's a start."

Mandy and James were in Joey's house. Joey's mother had gone into Walton, the nearby town, to spend the morning doing some shopping, so Mandy, James and Joey were taking the opportunity to give Scruff some training.

Mandy stared down at Scruff, who was

wagging his tail as if he knew he was about to learn something new, and was looking forward to it. "Now, how shall we organise his next lesson?"

"What are we going to teach him next?" Joey asked.

"To tell you when the front-door bell is ringing, I think," Mandy said.

"Would it be best if we showed Scruff how it should be done first?" James asked.

Mandy nodded. "That's a good idea," she said. "Otherwise he won't know how things are supposed to go."

"So . . ." James said slowly, working it out in his head. "I'll go outside and ring the doorbell. You sit in here with Joey, and when you hear the bell, you just get up to answer it."

"Right!" Mandy said.

She and Joey settled themselves down in the sitting-room with a book each, with Scruff sitting at Joey's feet. James went outside and a moment later the doorbell rang.

"Oh, I hear the bell," Mandy said for Scruff's benefit. "I'd better go and answer it."

She got up, went to the door and let James in.

Next it was James's turn to sit with Joey, while Mandy went outside and the whole thing was repeated.

All back in the sitting-room, Mandy perched on the arm of the sofa. "What did Scruff do when I rang? Did he look up at all?" she asked.

James nodded. "He looked up – and he gave a little bark. Nothing else."

Mandy bent down to ruffle his fur. "So now let's try not answering the door and see what he does."

They tried this, with James going outside first. This time, when she heard James ringing the bell, Mandy didn't move. She stayed exactly where she was, pretending to read.

Scruff pricked up his ears, and then looked at both Mandy and Joey and gave a short woof. As the two humans didn't seem bothered by the ringing of the doorbell, though, neither did he. He gave a yawn and put his head on his paws.

James rang again. And again and again. In the end, Mandy went to let him in.

"That doesn't seem to be working," Mandy said. "Scruff just doesn't seem to know what to do."

"Well," James said, "it's an awful lot for him to think about, isn't it? And it did take him loads of times on the green before he got that right."

"But he learned in the end!" Joey put in.

"Of course he did," said Mandy.

"I think we ought to go back to basics for a while," James said. "We ought to show Scruff a few more times that when the bell rings someone has to go and answer it."

Mandy and Joey thought this was the best thing too, so James went outside and rang the bell again. Mandy made a big thing of hearing it this time, saying to Joey and Scruff, "There's someone at the front door." Then Mandy, Joey and Scruff all went to answer it together.

They did this three times. Then James went outside again and rang the bell, and Mandy just sat there, not saying a word. She looked hard at Scruff, urging him to move. Apart from pricking up his ears, though, he didn't budge. The doorbell had rung so often that he'd even stopped woofing at it.

Finally, Mandy went to get James in. They had the orange juice and biscuits that Mrs Appleyard had left for them and had a rethink.

"Maybe," Mandy said, remembering to face Joey, "Scruff won't do it while *we're* here — you and me, James. Maybe he somehow knows that, if the door really needed answering, then one of us would do it."

James nodded. "That makes sense," he said.

Joey nodded too. "How about if we try it with me sitting on my own, then?"

Mandy finished her orange juice. "Yes," she said, "let's give that a try."

This time, James took his book into the kitchen and sat up at the breakfast bar, reading, while Mandy went outside. Joey and Scruff sat, as before, in the sitting-room.

Mandy stood on the front doorstep and rang the bell, loud and long. Nothing happened. She waited a moment and rang again. And again. Still nothing happened.

She was just about to ring once more

when, further up the road, she spotted her mother coming out of a house. She was carrying her big leather vet's bag.

Mandy ran towards her, waving. "Mum! What are you doing here?"

Her mother smiled. "I've just delivered four kittens," she said. "Two black, one white and one tabby."

"You had to deliver them?" Mandy asked. "I thought cats always did that for themselves."

"They do usually," her mother said, "but this time the first one got stuck. Luckily I managed to turn it round in time with no harm done."

"Four kittens!" Mandy said. "Can I go and see them?"

"You wouldn't want to see them at the moment," her mother said. "They don't look very pretty. More like little rats."

"I like little rats!" said Mandy.

Her mother laughed. "I know you do," she said, "and I'm sure Mrs Cobbold will let you see them later, when their eyes are open."

She opened her car door. "So how's your dog-training session going?"

"Oh!" Mandy said. "I forgot! I'm supposed to be on doorbell duty. Joey and James will wonder what's happened to me."

"Off you go, then, love," her mother said. "See you at lunch-time."

She waved and drove off, and Mandy

walked back to Joey's house, arriving in time to see a very indignant-looking Mrs Ponsonby coming back down Joey's path.

"I've rung and rung that bell," she said to Mandy, "but no one's answering. There's someone in there, though! I can see them through the window."

"Oh, Mrs Ponsonby, hang on!" Mandy began.

"I really can't hang on," the good lady said. "I haven't got all day. I merely called to welcome our newcomers to Welford, but if they—"

"Hello. Can I help?" Mrs Appleyard came through the gate carrying three bulging carrier bags. "Is there something wrong?"

"Well," Mrs Ponsonby said, "if you call not answering the door when someone's at home wrong, then there is!"

Mrs Appleyard looked confused. "Oh – well, the children are inside playing, so I can't think—" she began.

"I can explain," Mandy said. "We're training Scruff, you see."

Mrs Ponsonby frowned. "It was you and two other children who were making such a racket on the green on Monday, wasn't it? Shrieking and shouting and carrying on . . ."

Mrs Appleyard put the bags of shopping down. "Is this true, Mandy? And was Joey involved?"

"Yes, but—"

"I mean, I can't think why they're just sitting in there, not answering the doorbell," Mrs Ponsonby began again. "I'm afraid I find it very rude!"

"Mrs Ponsonby!" Mandy said in a rush. "We're trying to train Scruff – Joey's dog. Joey can't hear, you see, so we want to train Scruff to answer the door."

Mrs Ponsonby frowned. "This all sounds most peculiar."

"And they thought it was me outside ringing the bell, so they didn't answer it and . . ."

"I think I see," Mrs Appleyard said. She put her key in the lock. "Please come in," she said to Mrs Ponsonby. "We can introduce ourselves properly and you can meet Joey."

Mrs Ponsonby looked at her watch. "I'm afraid I haven't got time now," she said, frowning slightly. "Some other morning, perhaps."

"Oh, but—" Mrs Appleyard began.

"Good day to you both!" Mrs Ponsonby said and, with a slight, rather regal wave of her hand, was gone.

"Oh dear," Mandy said to Mrs Appleyard. "Sorry."

Mrs Appleyard sighed. "Not a very good way to meet the locals, was it? And it's all that dog's fault!"

8

Bad news

"Pretty Polly . . . pretty Polly," Mandy said encouragingly to the parrot, whose cage was now on the reception desk.

Jean looked at Polly. "That bird!" she said. "She never speaks when you want her to. She'll wait until I'm right in the middle of an important telephone conversation, though, and then start squawking at the top of her lungs."

Mandy giggled.

"She's going home today, anyway," Jean went on, "and I can't say I'm sorry."

"Did Mum and Dad find out what was wrong with her?"

Jean nodded. "It was mites under her feathers. Your dad has given her an injection and some insect powder. That should stop her losing any more."

"Poor Polly!" Mandy said.

"It was lucky that she didn't turn out to be bald Polly," Jean said. She closed the appointments book she'd been writing in. "So, what sort of a half-term are you having, Mandy? How's Scruff's training programme coming along?"

"Not *too* bad," Mandy said cautiously.

The day after the incident with Mrs Ponsonby, Mandy and Joey and James had tried the front-door bell trick again. After half an hour's hard work they thought that Scruff had almost got the idea – but then Mrs Appleyard, irritated by the constant ringing of the doorbell, had put a stop to the lessons. They were going to try again that afternoon.

The door from the street opened just then, and a man came in to deliver a parcel. He was about to go out again when his eye was caught by a poster on the notice-board.

"I recognise that dog!" he said suddenly, pointing at James and Mandy's poster for Scruff.

Mandy's heart jolted. She stared at the man in horror.

"That's the Browns' dog!" he went on.

Jean shot a sympathetic glance at Mandy. "The Browns' dog?" she asked. "Are they a local family?"

"They live near Walton. They rent the house next door to the garage."

"Are you sure?" Mandy asked him.

"Sure as eggs are eggs. I know the dog, see, because I've got one that looks pretty much the same. I take my car into that garage sometimes and I've seen him on the doorstep, or sitting in the front garden."

"Oh," Mandy said, dismayed.

"But do you know if they've actually lost a dog?" Jean asked.

"Dunno about that," the man said. "I haven't been over that way for a couple of months. I'm sure it belongs to them, though." He pushed open the door. "Expect they'll be pleased to get it back!"

Mandy swallowed hard.

"Yes. I'm . . . er . . . sure they will," Jean said. "We'll make some inquiries straight away."

"Glad to help!" said the man cheerfully as he went out. "I know what it's like when you lose a pet."

As the door swung shut behind him, Mandy and Jean looked at each other.

"Oh dear," Jean said sympathetically.

Mandy's eyes filled with tears. "Poor Joey," she said. "And poor Scruff." She bit her lip, "I suppose we—"

Jean shook her head. "Of course not," she said. "Don't even think about it." She patted Mandy's hand. "There may be someone in that Brown family who loves Scruff just as much as Joey does. Someone who may be missing him dreadfully."

Mandy nodded and gulped, but couldn't speak.

Jean got out the local telephone directory. "I'd better see if I can find the Browns' number and give them a ring." She patted Mandy's hand again. "Perhaps you'd better warn your friend Joey, just in case."

Just then, the door from the surgery swung open and Mandy's mother came out. "If there are no urgent calls for me, I thought I'd—" She saw Mandy's face and stopped. "What's wrong, Mandy?" she asked.

Jean explained and Mrs Hope gave Mandy a hug. "I know it's hard, but I think we ought to get this sorted out straight away," she said.

Mandy sniffed. "Right now?"

"The sooner the better," said Mrs Hope. "I was going over to Walton to do some shopping, anyway. If you come with me we'll stop at the house. Make quite sure it's the same dog."

Mandy sighed miserably. "OK."

"And, darling – you'd better bring one of the posters," said Mrs Hope.

Mandy was quiet on the journey to Walton. In one way she wanted to get there quickly and find out the worst, but in another way she dreaded arriving there at all. The thought that she might be reuniting someone with their pet didn't make her feel much better – not when she also knew how much Joey loved Scruff. It would be so hard for them to be parted . . .

Mrs Hope decided to fill up with petrol at the garage. "Then we'll leave the car here while we knock at the door of the Browns' house," she said. She glanced at Mandy. "It's best to know now, Mandy. The longer Joey has to get fond of Scruff, the harder it will be to say goodbye."

Mandy nodded silently. She knew this, of course, but it all seemed so unfair.

Scruff loved Joey and Joey loved him back. Joey needed Scruff, too. Needed him to watch out for him and protect him and be his ears . . .

As Mrs Hope drove into the garage, Mandy's eyes were fixed on the house just beyond it: a square, modern building with a red front door and a rather unkempt garden. Had they or hadn't they lost a dog? That was the question.

Five minutes later, Mandy and her mother were making their way up the front path. Mrs Hope knocked and two or three dogs began barking. A pleasant-looking young woman came to the door.

"Mrs Brown?" Mandy's mother asked, while Mandy crossed all her fingers and wished with all her might.

The woman shook her head. "No, I'm sorry," she said. "The Browns have moved down to Brighton."

"Oh!" Mrs Hope hesitated. "Did they move out very long ago?"

"They've been gone about six weeks, I think. The house was empty for a couple of weeks, and then we moved in. Is there something I can help you with?"

Mrs Hope explained about Scruff, and Mandy showed her the poster with the photo of him.

The woman looked at it carefully. "Well, I don't know whether this will be good news or bad news for you, but that *is* their dog."

Mandy's heart started beating fast.

"I know, because they left the poor little chap behind!" she continued. "Apparently they were going to a flat in

Brighton, where they couldn't keep a pet – so they just left him!"

"You're joking!" Mrs Hope said. "That's disgraceful."

"I agree entirely," said the woman. "We fed him for a couple of days, but we've got dogs of our own and couldn't take another one in. We were about to ring the RSPCA when he disappeared – just vanished into thin air. I had no idea where he went."

Mandy and her mother exchanged looks.

"We know where!" Mandy said, feeling so happy that she could have turned a cartwheel on the spot.

"Well, I hope it's a better home than he had with the Browns'," said the woman. "Imagine just abandoning him here!"

"Oh, he has got a better home," said Mandy. "A much better home!"

9
Clever dog

"Yes!"

"He's done it!"

"Good boy, Scruff!"

Mandy, James and Joey jumped round the startled dog in delight. Joey opened a packet of doggy chocdrops and put a little pile on the floor in front of him.

"You clever dog!" he said, picking

him up and hugging him.

Scruff, who'd already seen the choc-drops, wriggled in Joey's arms. He couldn't see what all the fuss was about! All that had happened was that someone had rung the bell, so he'd alerted Joey and led him to the door. Easy!

"And all without really trying!" Mandy said.

She and James had turned up at Joey's house and rung the bell as usual, thinking that Mrs Appleyard was in. She wasn't – but Scruff was!

"He must have remembered all his training from the other mornings," James said.

Mandy nodded. "Suddenly it all made sense to him."

"He's the cleverest dog in the world!" Joey said, hugging Scruff as he cleared the last few treats from the carpet.

Joey rolled on to the floor with Scruff, and the dog took some playful nips at Joey's sweatshirt, pulling it with his teeth. Joey pulled it back again and Scruff growled and pretended to bite the material, acting as if the sweat-shirt was alive and he was pouncing on it.

Mandy and James were just watching this and laughing when Mrs Appleyard appeared.

"Whatever's going on?" she said, looking alarmed. "Is that dog attacking Joey?"

Mandy quickly lifted Scruff off Joey. "They were just having a tussle," she said.

Mrs Appleyard frowned. "Is that what you call it? It sounded dreadful. Are you all right, Joey?"

Joey scrambled to his feet. "I'm fine, Mum. And you'll never guess what we've got to show you . . ."

Mrs Appleyard frowned again. "What's that on the carpet, Joey? Chocolate?"

Joey hastily rubbed at the mark with the cuff of his sweat-shirt. "Just wait, Mum. You're going to be surprised. Very surprised."

"Am I really?" she said. "I suppose it's something to do with that dog."

"If you go outside again, we'll show you," said Mandy.

"But I've only just come in," Mrs Appleyard objected. "I want to put the groceries away."

"You've just got to come outside with me and Mandy for two minutes," James pleaded.

"It's really brilliant, Mum!" said Joey.

At last Mrs Appleyard agreed. She, Mandy and James went outside, shutting the front door firmly behind them.

"We need to wait for a little while," Mandy said.

"Just to allow Scruff to settle down," added James.

Mrs Appleyard looked bemused as Mandy and James counted under their breath.

"Forty nine . . . fifty!" Mandy said. She turned to Mrs Appleyard. "Now will you ring the doorbell, please?"

"Well, that won't be any good, will it?" said Mrs Appleyard. "Why don't I just use my key to get in?"

James shook his head. "It's all part of the surprise," he said.

Mrs Appleyard shrugged, but rang the bell anyway.

A moment later Joey, accompanied by Scruff, opened the door.

"Yes?" he said, beaming at his mother. "Did you ring?"

Mrs Appleyard looked stunned. "How did you know when I rang?" she asked.

"Scruff told me!" Joey said proudly. "He heard the bell and he tapped me on the foot and led me to the door."

"Yes, but—"

"And before you say anything, I only opened it because I knew it was you!" Joey said. "I wouldn't open it to just anyone."

"Of course not," Mrs Appleyard said, still looking stunned. She shook her head in amazement. "Well," she said, "that's just marvellous!" She stared down at Scruff and put out a hand as if she was going to pat him, but pulled it away suddenly. "I suppose we've got Mandy and James to thank for this, have we?" she asked.

"And Joey and Scruff," Mandy put in.

"Will he do it again?"

"Any time you like!" said Mandy.

"Let's see the full trick, then," Mrs Appleyard said. "And can I stay inside with Joey this time?"

"Of course you can," Mandy said.

Smiling broadly, Joey went back into the sitting-room with Scruff. Mandy and Mrs Appleyard went into the kitchen, and James went outside.

After a few moments he rang the bell

and Mrs Appleyard peeped round the kitchen door. As she saw Joey going off to answer it, a big smile lit up her face.

"I can hardly believe it," she said when everyone was together again. "You must all have worked really hard to train him."

"So can I definitely keep him now?" Joey pleaded. "You wouldn't send him away now, would you?"

"Well, I—" Mrs Appleyard began.

"And we do know now that he doesn't belong to anyone else," Joey said persuasively, for Mandy's mum had already telephoned to tell Mrs Appleyard what they'd discovered about Scruff's former owners.

Mrs Appleyard looked down at Scruff. "He certainly seems all right, but I did say two weeks' trial, didn't I? He's not been living here a week yet."

"Oh, but *Mum* . . . " Joey began.

"That's enough, darling," Mrs Apple-yard said. "So far, so good. But it's still too early to say for sure."

10

Doggy disgrace

James came round to Animal Ark after lunch. He had Blackie with him and they were going to call for Joey and Scruff. They wanted the two dogs to get to know each other really well, so they were going to take them on a long walk up to Beacon Point and back.

Mandy had borrowed a collar and lead

from the surgery for Scruff, who hadn't yet got a set of his own. Mrs Appleyard had said that she'd buy him a new collar and lead when his two weeks' trial was up.

As Mandy closed the door of her house behind her, Blackie leaped upon her, almost knocking her sideways.

"Down, boy!" James said. "Get down, you naughty thing!"

He put Blackie on his lead. "Maybe when Blackie sees how well Scruff is behaving, some of it will rub off on him," he said.

Mandy ruffled Blackie's ears. "He's not that bad. He's still a puppy, really."

"I think he'll *always* be a puppy," James said, trying to hold Blackie back as they walked along.

When they got to Joey's house, Mrs Appleyard told them that Joey was playing in the garden with Scruff. They went round to the back and Blackie and Scruff ran up to each other, both of them bounding with excitement at the thought

of playing together. They'd met twice before and had got on well. Blackie was much bigger than Scruff, of course, and between them they'd invented a game where Scruff ran under Blackie's legs and Blackie turned round and round in circles trying to catch him.

When they'd had enough of that, Joey brought out two bowls of water. Blackie gulped all his down, then pushed his nose into Scruff's bowl and finished that off, too.

Mandy, James and Joey decided to set

off on their walk. Scruff sat quietly while they put the borrowed collar on him, and Mandy had just given Joey the lead so he could fix that on, when they heard the front-door bell ring. Then came the noise of a dog yapping.

Before they could grab Scruff, he was up and running, fast as a greyhound, towards where the yapping was coming from.

"What's happening?" said Joey, who hadn't heard a thing. "Why did he run off like that?"

"He heard a dog barking," Mandy explained. "From the front of the house." Just as she spoke there came the horrible noise of two dogs yowling and snarling at each other, then someone shouting.

"Sounds like a fight!" James said fearfully. He touched Joey's arm. "Let's go!"

They hurried round to the front of the house, where they could see Joey's mum standing in the doorway. Outside on the step stood Mrs Ponsonby, who'd just snatched up her Pekinese, Pandora. At her feet stood a fierce Scruff, looking up at Pandora and barking madly.

Mrs Appleyard turned to see Joey and his friends. "Come and get this dog at once!" she cried.

Mandy quickly turned to face Joey. "You'd better go and get Scruff!" she pointed.

Joey ran forward and picked up Scruff, who just yapped once more and was quiet.

"Disgraceful!" Mrs Ponsonby said, as her dog continued to bark. "That dog attacked us for no good reason."

"He just appeared out of nowhere," Mrs Appleyard said, all flustered. "Really, I can't apologise enough, Mrs Ponsonby."

"People really ought to keep their dogs under control," Mrs Ponsonby said. "Upsetting my Pandora like that . . ."

"I really am very sorry," Mrs Appleyard went on. "I don't know what's the matter with him. He didn't actually hurt

your dog though, did he? Just made a lot of noise."

"He frightened Pandora to death!"

"Oh, but he was just defending his territory," Mandy said, feeling that she couldn't keep quiet a moment longer. "He thought Pandora was a threat. He was defending us."

Mrs Appleyard frowned. "Well, the other dog in the garden – your Blackie – didn't feel the need to leap at Pandora, did he? He's still sitting there quietly."

"That's because it wasn't his territory that was being threatened," Mandy explained.

"And anyway, Scruff was just barking," Joey argued. "He wouldn't have hurt anyone."

"We're not sure of that," Mrs Appleyard said. She took a deep breath. "I really can't risk having our visitors threatened in this way."

She turned her attention to Mrs Ponsonby and smiled rather shakily. "But won't you come in?" she said. "We can have a nice peaceful cup of tea in the sitting-room."

"How kind," said Mrs Ponsonby and, holding Pandora aloft like a precious piece of china, she entered the house.

Mandy, James and Joey followed Mrs Appleyard into the kitchen.

"Honestly, Scruff wouldn't hurt a fly," Mandy said anxiously. "And we're going to teach him to alert Joey to alarm-bells next!" said James.

Joey just looked at his mother,

concerned and waiting to see what she was going to say.

Mrs Appleyard filled the kettle with water and then turned to face Joey. "I'm sorry, darling," she said, "I don't think we can keep him."

Joey gave a little cry.

"I can't have a dog like that around. I don't know what he's going to do next. I just wouldn't feel safe."

Tears filled Joey's eyes. "But—" he began.

"I'm sorry, Joey," his mother said, "but I've made up my mind. He can stay for the weekend, but after that you'll have to find him a new home."

"Oh, Mum . . ."

"And that's absolutely final, I'm afraid."

11

Scruff to the rescue

"It's just so sad," Mandy said to her gran later that day in Lilac Cottage. "I mean, Scruff wouldn't have hurt Pandora, he really wouldn't. He was just being noisy."

"I know, love," Gran said. "Some dogs – well, it's true what they say, isn't it? – their bark is worse than their bite."

Mandy nodded slowly.

Gran tutted. "It is very sad, though. Especially as you were getting on so well with Scruff's training." She poured Mandy a glass of orange juice. "What will happen to him now?"

Mandy sighed heavily. "Mum and Dad said that the animal sanctuary will take him."

Gran nodded. "They'll find a good home for him there."

"But he's already *got* a good home," said Mandy. She sighed again. "Oh, I do wish Mrs Ponsonby hadn't come round just then – when we were in the garden. She always makes a mess of things. Or that she'd come round without Pandora. Or that—"

"Now, don't upset yourself," Gran said. "Why don't you go into the garden and get Grandad to pick you the last of the runner-beans to take home with you?"

Mandy looked embarrassed. "Thank you very much, but Dad said he's eaten all the beans he can possibly manage. He said to tell you that he thinks he's changing into a runner-bean!"

Gran chuckled. "To tell you the truth, I'm a little bit fed up with them myself. I've already got twenty bags in the deep-freeze. At this rate, we won't need to plant any next year."

"Anyway, I'm on my way round to James's house now," Mandy went on. "And then we're going to visit Joey and try and cheer him up a bit. James says he's going to let him have a share in Blackie."

"That's nice of James," Gran said warmly. "Though I can't see that young scamp of a pup learning to be a hearing dog!"

"Neither can I," Mandy said. "That's why Scruff was so brilliant . . ."

Gran gave her a hug. "Now, remember! No gloomy faces in front of Joey. He's going to need cheering up more than you."

Mandy managed a smile. "I know, Gran. And I'll try to be cheerful when we get there, really I will . . ."

★ ★ ★

Mandy and James were solemn and silent, deep in thought, as they walked along the High Street towards Joey's house. It was only as they got near to the post office that James spoke.

"Maybe we should get Joey some sweets or something," he said.

"Good idea." Mandy nodded in agreement. "It might make him feel a bit better."

"It might . . ." James said, "but I don't think so. I know how I'd feel if my mum said I had to get rid of Blackie."

Mandy shook her head. "Poor Joey," she said.

"And poor Scruff," put in James.

They went into the post office to buy some sweets, and were coming out when Mandy suddenly caught hold of James's arm.

"There's Joey now!" she said, pointing up the road. "Walking up towards the green."

They quickened their pace to try and

catch up with Joey, knowing that it
would be useless calling to him.

"It looks as if he's already been trying
to cheer himself up," James said. "He's
bought himself an ice cream."

"And there's Scruff trotting along
behind him!" Mandy said.

As Mandy spoke, a car came from the
direction of the green and began to make

its way towards the High Street. It was going very fast.

Just then, too, Joey, intent on his ice cream and feeling so miserable that he wasn't thinking about what he was doing, took a step off the pavement.

The car hooted its horn loudly. But Joey didn't hear it and took another step forward. Mandy clutched James's arm in fright.

"Joey!" Mandy cried, and she and James started running down the street.

The car hooted again, long and loud, then there was a terrific screech of brakes as it tried to stop. Just then Scruff, who had heard Mandy call Joey's name, took a flying leap at Joey's ankle and held on to his jeans with his teeth.

Joey fell over, on to his ice cream, and the car came to a juddering halt sideways across the road. By the time Mandy and James arrived, panting, Mrs Appleyard – who'd been coming out of the post office – and three other people, had arrived at the scene.

Joey was helped to his feet and Mrs Appleyard clutched him tightly. "What were you *doing*? You crossed the road without looking, didn't you?" she said, and then she burst into tears, hugging Joey for all she was worth. Joey wriggled uncomfortably, feeling that he could hardly breathe.

The driver of the car got out. "Silly kid," he muttered.

"You were going too fast!" one of the bystanders said accusingly.

"That boy wasn't looking where he was going!" the car driver retorted.

Joey, who was looking bewildered, shook his head. "No, I wasn't," he said. "I was eating my ice cream and thinking about poor Scruff . . ."

Mandy took a tissue out of her pocket and wiped some ice cream from Joey's jeans. "Are you all right?" she said. "We saw it — James and I saw everything. Scruff heard me shout your name and he saved you!"

Joey, suddenly realising exactly what

119

had happened, struggled out of his mother's arms. "Scruff!" he said, looking round frantically for his dog. "Scruff saved me!"

Scruff was intent on licking dollops of ice cream from anywhere he could, and didn't even look up.

Mrs Appleyard, white-faced, nodded. "Yes, that's right – I saw it, too. He did save your life!"

"That dog's a hero!" one of the onlookers remarked.

The little drama over, the people who'd gathered at the scene went on their way. The car driver, after making sure Joey was all right and muttering a few more words about it not being his fault, got back in his car and drove off.

Mandy, James, Joey and his mum just stood there, looking down at Scruff.

"Scruff's a hero," Joey said.

"Yes, he is," Mandy agreed.

Joey looked up at his mum. "So do you think I can keep him, Mum?"

Mrs Appleyard couldn't seem to stop

hugging Joey. "Yes . . . you can, darling," she said. "How could we ever get rid of him now?" She straightened up and took a deep breath. "Now, why don't we all go into the pet shop in Walton and buy Scruff a collar and lead of his own. And a basket and anything else you think he might need. You'd know about things like that, Mandy, wouldn't you?"

Mandy nodded, her eyes shining.

Joey picked up Scruff and buried his face in his fur. "I can keep you!" he said. "You're mine forever!"

And Scruff licked Joey's face, as if to say that suited him just fine!